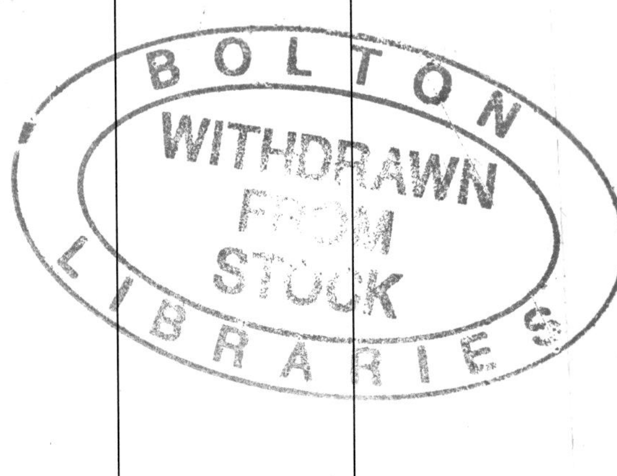

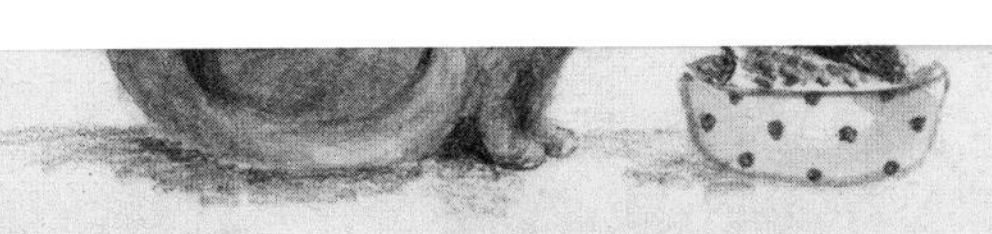

Also by the Author:

Alfie Cat in Trouble

For Adult Readers:

Alfie the Doorstep Cat

A Cat Called Alfie

Alfie and George – Coming soon!

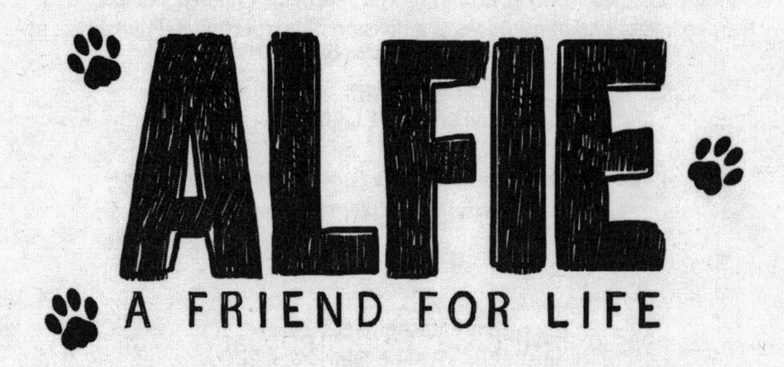

Far from Home

RACHEL WELLS

Illustrations by Katie May Green

HarperCollins *Children's Books*

First published in Great Britain by HarperCollins *Children's Books* 2016
HarperCollins *Children's Books* is a division of HarperCollins*Publishers* Ltd,
HarperCollins *Publishers*,
1 London Bridge Street,
London SE1 9GF

The HarperCollins *Children's Books* website address is
www.harpercollins.co.uk

1

ISBN 978-0-00-817205-3

Printed and bound in England by
Clays Ltd, St Ives plc

To my gorgeous Godson, Eric

My name is Alfie and I am a cat, or more accurately I am a doorstep cat. This means I have one main family who I live with in Edgar Road, but I also visit other homes. I am a bit like a part-time pet in each one. I get fed (yummy), I get stroked and fussed over and I also get to play with lots of children. I really like children. I have many friends, both human and cat, but my latest are the Clover family. They recently moved into the next street to me and I have been spending a bit of time with them.

You see, I also get involved in the lives of

my humans, who often need my help. And this cat is very good at helping people. It's what I do – what any good doorstep cat should do.

Chapter One

I sat on the pavement with the Clover family. Eight-year-old Stanley squealed excitedly as they stared at a van.

'We actually get to live in there?' He was looking more unruly than usual, hair messy, T-shirt back to front and the laces of his trainers untied. I needed to give that boy a lesson in grooming – I always made sure my blue-grey fur looked its best. Mind you, his parents were a bit scruffy too. Only Viola was neat and tidy.

'Yes, dear, it's our camper van,' Mrs Clover said. 'We're sleeping in it at the campsite.' The Clovers were going on holiday. 'Right, well children, chop chop, we must finish packing.'

'I'll miss you, Alfie,' Stanley said, picking me up. I purred. I would miss the Clovers too.

As Stanley put me down, he and Mr Clover went back into the house.

'Come along, dear,' Mrs Clover said. Viola looked glum. 'Whatever is wrong? Don't you want to go on holiday?'

'No, I mean yes, I really do. Oh, it doesn't matter,' Viola sighed as she hurried after her mum.

After they'd gone, I decided to look around the house on wheels. I climbed in through an open window and my eyes widened. There was a small kitchen area, a room with a toilet, and a table with bench seats round it. Being a cat, I wasn't sure where they would sleep, but I assumed they would work that out.

The sun streamed through one of the windows. Tucked down the side of the bench was a cushion. It was a perfect spot, so

I thought I'd just enjoy a bit of sunbathing before the Clovers left.

I opened my eyes slowly, blinked, yawned and stretched. I felt my stomach lurch as I became aware of motion. I was moving. How was I moving? I sat up but didn't recognise my surroundings, so I jumped up and looked out of a window – I could see flashes of trees whizzing past. Yikes! I was in the van! I wasn't meant to be here!

'YELP!'

'Alfie?' Viola said.

I looked and saw Viola and Stanley sitting at a pull-out table, playing a game. Mr Clover was driving, Mrs Clover sat next to him.

'Oh yikes,' Stanley said. 'Alfie, what are you doing here?'

'Miaow.' Obviously I'd fallen asleep and woken up in a moving house. Oh well, no problem, they couldn't have gone far.

'We've been driving for three hours,' Viola said.

Three hours?

She bit her lip. 'Mum?' Carefully, she moved nearer the front.

'Yes, dear?'

'It seems that Alfie has accidentally stowed away.'

'What? WHAT? Dear, stop the van, we have to stop the van. STOP.'

'Oh goodness, oh goodness.'

Whilst Mr and Mrs Clover panicked, I started cleaning myself. I couldn't believe I'd been asleep all that time.

'Dad, just pull over when it's safe,'

Viola said sensibly.

A few minutes later, Mr Clover found a lay-by.

'We'll just have to go home,' Mr Clover said.

'But we're nearly there!' Viola pointed out.

'Then we at least need to phone Alfie's family,' Mrs Clover said. 'The number's on his collar.'

'Yes, let's phone them. That's exactly what we'll do,' Mr Clover said.

'But then what?' Mrs Clover asked.

'Just explain we're in Devon and that Alfie will have to come on holiday with us for a week,' Viola suggested.

'But a cat, on holiday. I mean whoever

heard of such a thing?' Mrs Clover shrieked.

Actually, I had been on holiday before, but I couldn't tell them that.

'Mum, Dad, calm down,' Stanley said.

Viola's plan sounded good to me. I'd miss my other families but a holiday might just be what the vet ordered.

'OK.' Mrs Clover calmed down and phoned my home. I was going on holiday!

For the rest of the journey, I was as excited as Stanley. Only Viola was quiet.

We stopped by a sign that said *Curly Wood Campsite* and were greeted by a man and a woman.

'Mr Clover and family.' Mr Clover got out of the van.

'Welcome to Curly Wood. I'm Mr Green the campsite manager, and this is my wife, Mrs Green.' The man who welcomed them was tall and thin with a funny moustache on his face which looked a bit like a slug. I hoped it wasn't a slug. The lady was wearing a tool belt.

'Thank you,' Mrs Clover said.

'I need to undertake a routine check of your vehicle,' said Mr Green. He pulled a book out of his shirt pocket.

'Oh, OK.' Mrs Clover looked unsure.

'Nice camper van.' He climbed in and came

face to face with me. He jumped; I put a paw up in greeting. 'A cat?'

'Yes, funny story, he sort of ended up here, we didn't mean to bring him—' Mr Clover explained.

'I don't think visiting cats are permitted on our campsite,' Mr Green said. 'We have a cat called Humphrey but he lives with us.' He began looking through his book. 'We do allow well-behaved dogs, although they must be kept on a lead at all times, but…' He scratched his head.

Dogs? Did I hear right? I wasn't sure I wanted to stay now.

'We promise he'll be no trouble,' Stanley said.

The man looked at him, took a whistle out of his pocket and blew it loudly. We all jumped.

'I'm looking through my rule book and I appreciate silence.'

After a while, he put the book back in his shirt pocket. 'I am not happy but unfortunately I can't find anything in the rule book about visiting cats. And I can't break the rules when enforcing the rules, so, against my wishes, he can stay.'

'Hooray,' Stanley said; he was silenced by a look.

'But one whiff of trouble and you'll be out.' Mr Green pointed his whistle at me. 'Enjoy your stay.' As he left the van, he asked Mrs Green to show us where to park.

We stood outside the van; we were going to look around the campsite.

'Alfie, you need to stay inside,' Mr Clover said, lifting me back in. 'We assured your family we'd take care of you and we can't risk you getting lost. Or worse,' he finished.

What could be worse than getting lost? Some holiday this was! But then I noticed an open window. When the coast was clear, I jumped out. There were tents, caravans and other camper vans and in the distance I could see the wood. It was lovely—

'Hisss.'

I stopped, turned and found myself staring at a plump ginger cat.

'Hello.' My legs trembled.

'What are you doing here?' he asked nastily.

I flashed him my most charming smile. 'I'm Alfie; it's very nice to meet you.'

'I said what are you doing here?'

'I accidentally came on holiday.'

I wondered if he would attack; he was huge.

'This is my campsite and I don't need the likes of you on it,' he said.

'Humphrey?' a woman's voice said. The cat softened as he turned round. 'Humphrey, it's teatime,' the voice repeated.

He narrowed his eyes at me then ran off.

I felt unsettled by my encounter so I went off in search of Stanley and Viola. I came across a small building and snuck in through an open door. Mr and Mrs Clover were sitting at a table with some other adults. I stalked, unobserved, to the back of the room and found Stanley and Viola. Stanley was laughing and joking; there were two other boys and a girl with them. Viola hung back – she seemed to be hiding behind her long hair. I wanted to go to her but Stanley spotted me first.

'Alfie,' he whispered, scooping me up and hiding me under his jacket. 'If anyone sees you, you'll be in trouble.'

'Who's that?' a boy asked.

'Alfie, our cat from home,' Stanley explained. "Well, not exactly our cat. You see, he is and he isn't.' I saw the other children look at Stanley in confusion. 'Oh, but that's a bit of a long story—'

'Hey, best not to let Uncle Green see him

in here,' the boy interrupted. 'Let's go outside, quick.'

The boy had an accent I hadn't heard before.

'Cute cat,' the girl whispered, as the smallest boy stood beside her. I saw Viola's cheeks redden as they did when she was around new people.

'Thank you,' she said quietly, with a smile.

She could be awfully shy, poor thing. I knew she was nervous about starting her new school when they got back too. I rubbed against her legs to offer support.

Stanley walked out with the boy and girl next to him and Viola went to follow, but Mrs

Clover stopped her.

'Ah, Viola, there you are. Mr Green has said you can see the piano now.'

'Piano?' said Viola.

'Yes, we found a campsite that had one,' her mother explained. 'So that you could practise while we were away.'

'Oh,' said Viola in a small voice.

It was clear that she wanted to come with us but, instead, she followed her mum to the piano.

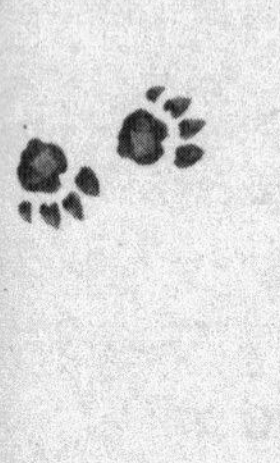

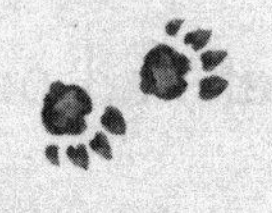

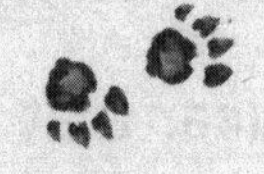

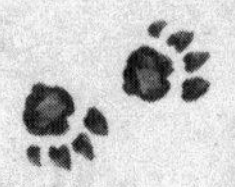

Chapter Two

As I wandered outside the following morning, I saw Humphrey glaring at me. 'Hi Humphrey.'

'You still here?' he replied.

'Well, I don't really have a choice,' I pointed out. 'It would be nice if we could be friends?'

I raised my whiskers hopefully.

'I already told you – I don't like other cats on my campsite.'

I was about to argue, but then rounding the corner were the three children from last night. I discovered, after Stanley had got me safely out of the clubhouse, that they were Nathan, Emily and Jack. Nathan was the oldest at twelve – he was staying with his uncle and aunt, Mr and Mrs Green. He had come from America, which was very far away. Emily and Jack were brother and sister. Emily was ten and Jack was seven. As soon as he spotted them, Humphrey changed; he was nice to children. Stanley stepped out of the van.

'Hey, Stan, meet Humphrey the campsite cat. He's really cool,' Nathan said.

I miaowed. I was cool too.

'Wow, he's big. Alfie and he can be friends,' Stanley said, picking me up.

'What are we going to do now?' Jack asked excitedly.

'There isn't a whole lot to do here,' Nathan said. 'My uncle sure likes his rules, but we can go to the playground, I guess.'

'Lead the way. I'm an adventurer and generally I can find adventures everywhere,' Stanley said confidently.

'Yay!' Jack said. I wasn't sure why.

'Vi, are you coming?' Stanley shouted into the van.

Viola emerged, smiled shyly at the others and they all set off. I started to follow.

'You're coming too?' Humphrey asked, not sounding thrilled.

'Yes, I'm an adventurer's cat, after all,' I replied huffily.

The playground had seen better days. There were a couple of swings, a slide which was scuffed and rusty, a roundabout which creaked when it moved and a see-saw.

'We don't have much to work with to make an adventure,' Stanley said as he surveyed it.

'I told you that, pal,' Nathan said, patting his shoulder.

Jack was on the swing, asking his sister to give him a push, and Viola, I noticed, hung back again. I went to rub myself against her legs, but then I spotted something under a nearby bush. Viola followed me as I dived under it.

'It's a football,' Viola said, as I nudged it to her with my nose.

'Nice one, Vi,' Stanley said. 'Right, we can make an assault course.'

'What's an assault course?' Jack asked, wide-eyed.

'It's like a race where we do different things.

'We can start the course here.' He walked towards some wooden stumps with a bench at the end. They were all different heights. 'Right, follow me!' he said as he climbed from the bench to the tallest one. 'It's going to be cool.' He excitedly explained to everyone how it would work. 'Right, let's go,' Stanley announced.

They took it in turns. They had to jump over the bars of the roundabout while the other

children spun it, then when a bit dizzy they had to stand on the swing and do ten swings without falling off; run across the see-saw, and finally walk up the slide with the football and then throw it between the swings, like a goal.

I had to admit it was impressive, although it didn't look safe.

'There'll be trouble,' Humphrey grumbled, coming up beside me.

'Why?' I asked.

'It's against the rules. Mr Green's rule book clearly states that the playground must only be used as it should be.'

'But he's not here,' I pointed out.

'Don't say I didn't warn you,' Humphrey replied before climbing a tree to watch. I thought about joining him but then I'm not exactly a fan of trees, having been stuck up one in the past, so I stayed on land.

The children were having a lovely time and

Viola started to smile at last. But then I heard, '*peep, peep, peep*'. The whistle was loud and a bit too close for comfort.

Jack, who had been *standing* on the swing, fell off. Emily and Viola rushed to him; he'd landed on his bottom.

'*Peep, peep, peep*. Just what do you think you are doing?' Mr Green shouted.

'Um, Uncle, we were just having a race,' Nathan explained.

'Nathan, you should know better. When we invited you to stay we expected you to obey the rules.' He pulled his book out. 'You have broken rules 77, 89, 111 and many more. I'll take that—' He snatched the football out of

Stanley's arms. 'Balls can only be played with in the designated ball area, rule 199.'

'Wow, he likes his rules,' Stanley said after he'd gone. I miaowed in agreement.

'Boy does he.' Nathan looked downcast. 'It's not like I even asked to come to stay. I was hoping to spend the summer back home in the US, playing with my friends, but no, because my parents were busy with work, I end up miles from home, in a caravan with Aunt and Uncle Green!'

'Sorry to hear that, mate.' Stanley squeezed Nathan's shoulder sympathetically.

'What shall we do now?' Jack asked. Viola looked at Emily but stayed silent.

'I know a real good trick,' Nathan said, suddenly grinning.

'What?' The others crowded round him.

'Follow me to the shower block and I'll show you.'

They all walked off and I made to follow them. I felt Humphrey come up beside me.

'Hiss,' he said.

'What?' I asked.

'This is not a good idea. Nathan's unhappy and I think he's looking for trouble.'

'What's the matter with him?' I asked, interested. I was a cat who always helped humans in trouble, after all.

'He's homesick. Poor kid got sent over here

because his parents are working away and he misses home.'

'That's something I have some experience of.' I explained about Stanley and Viola and how I'd accidentally ended up in the van.

'We'd better go and keep an eye on them; this isn't going to end well.' He bounded off and I followed him.

Nathan led them to the back of the shower block. He giggled as the others watched him turn a big tap. Four people, wrapped in towels, heads covered in shampoo, ran out screaming.

'It's freezing,' someone cried.

'The water's gone cold,' someone else

shouted. Lots of voices shrieked all at once.

'You did that?' Viola asked. She looked cross. Nathan fell about laughing.

'But we'll get into trouble,' Emily said. Jack looked as if he might cry.

'Run,' Stanley said; they all ran. I heard the whistle and Mr Green rounded the corner, blowing it furiously. Angry people crowded round him as he tried to pacify them, with Humphrey at his feet.

I found the children sitting outside our van. None of them looked happy.

'What did you do that for?' Stanley demanded. 'We could have got into big trouble.'

'I don't know; sometimes I just can't help myself,' Nathan admitted. 'I guess I did it because I miss home.'

'But getting us into trouble isn't going to help you,' Stanley pointed out.

'Sorry,' he mumbled.

'Look, we need to have fun but not get into too much trouble. I know, I have a lot of experience of trouble,' Stanley said. He did.

'What can we do now?' Jack asked.

'We can play table tennis – there's a table in a room by the clubhouse. We're allowed,' Nathan said.

'Yay!' Jack was excited again. As they stood up, Mrs Clover appeared.

'Viola, it's time for piano practice – come along.'

Viola looked sadly at the other children as they all ran off.

'But—' she started.

'Chop chop, Viola,' her mother said.

'I'll never make friends at this rate,' I heard her mumble.

'What, dear?' Mrs Clover asked.

'Nothing, Mum,' Viola sighed.

Chapter Three

Viola was still unhappy the following morning. And no one but me seemed to notice. Mr Clover was loving the fresh air; Mrs Clover was drawing – something she said she never normally had time for. Stanley was happy – all the children were going on a campsite treasure hunt, and he enjoyed being with his new friends. I needed to do something for Viola – it seemed I was her only chance.

The children waited by the clubhouse. Jack was bouncing around, Emily hung back, a bit like Viola – they were so alike they could have been friends, if only one of them would speak! I felt my fur tingle as an idea started coming to me.

'Guys, listen up. This treasure hunt sucks,' Nathan said.

'What does *sucks* mean?' Jack asked.

'It means it's rubbish,' Stanley explained –

being an adventurer in training meant he was good at international languages.

'Yeah, it's rubbish. The prize is some dumb candy.'

'What's candy?' Jack asked.

'Sweets,' Stanley said.

'So, anyway, here's my plan. How about we all pretend not to understand the clues? It'll be so funny,' Nathan suggested.

'That does sound funny,' Stanley said.

'Will we get into trouble?' Viola asked.

'Nah, Uncle Green will just think we're stupid,' Nathan said.

'But I really like sweets.' Jack sounded upset.

'You can get candy anytime but this will be more fun, trust me,' Nathan said.

I miaowed – it sounded strange to me – like it could get them into BIG trouble. They really shouldn't trust him.

'But, but—' Jack looked as if he might cry. Emily put her hand on his shoulder.

'Great, so we're all agreed. This will be so cool.' Nathan gave all the children a high-five.

Mr Green approached with a girl I hadn't seen before. She was about Stanley's age, with dark hair in bunches and wearing dungarees.

'Ah, you are all here,' Mr Green said, blowing his whistle. 'I do like punctuality. Come on, line up, line up.'

‘I’m Poppy,’ the new girl said. Stanley and Nathan looked at each other, about to tell her what they were up to, but Nathan put his finger to his lip.

‘Yes, sorry, this is Poppy. Her family just arrived so luckily she is just in time for the treasure hunt.’ He blew his whistle again. ‘Not only do we get some fresh air but also we get to exercise the grey matter.’

‘What?’ Jack looked terrified. I thought he probably wouldn’t have to pretend not to get the clues.

‘Your brain,’ Emily explained as Mr Green set off.

I followed them, trying to keep myself

hidden from Mr Green. I wasn't sure if cats were allowed on the treasure hunt. I was pretty sure I wasn't.

'Right, first clue. What has leaves but isn't a tree?' Mr Green asked.

'A table?' Nathan asked. Stanley giggled behind his hand.

'No, try again,' Mr Green said. They were standing by the bush which I was hiding under, and as I saw a piece of paper, I realised the answer. I tried to hide myself further as I saw Poppy's hand reach in and retrieve the clue.

'A plant! I've got it!' she said triumphantly.

'Well done, Poppy. At least someone here

has some sense,' Mr Green muttered. As Nathan smirked at Stanley, I saw the girls exchange a look. They didn't seem happy. 'Right, on we go. I have pegs but I don't hang washing,' Mr Green said.

'A—' Viola started to say, but Stanley pushed her out of the way. 'Ahh,' she said, nearly falling on me.

'I'm not sure I understand. What do you mean by pegs?' Stanley asked. 'Is it actual washing?'

'Well done for trying, Stanley, but no.' Mr Green sounded kind. Viola turned pink and Emily looked at the floor. This wasn't funny. Not at all.

‘A tent!’ Poppy shouted triumphantly, and she ran round the tents until she found one with a clue pinned to it. She handed the clue to Mr Green.

‘Well done again, Poppy. I really can’t understand why no one else can get the clues.’ Mr Green scratched his head and looked puzzled. Nathan smiled again, and although he hadn’t welcomed me with open arms, I felt very sorry for Mr Green.

‘Ah, this is a good one. Right, what is a cat’s favourite food?’ Mr Green looked hopeful, but the boys looked blankly at him. Viola and Emily were clearly uncomfortable and I knew the answer! Pilchards. Not that I knew where to find them. I only wished I did!

'Cat food,' Nathan said. Mr Green shook his head.

'Is it fish?' Poppy asked, running towards the shop. The other children watched as she went to the tins of fish and found a clue underneath them. 'Got it!'

Mr Green looked relieved, and quickly carried on. But the next clues were equally embarrassing. Mr Green patted Poppy's head each time she got the clues whilst the other children looked blank.

'Right, last clue. Beneath the house that isn't a house,' Mr Green announced. 'Let's see if someone other than Poppy can get this one.'

‘I don’t understand,’ Nathan said. I was feeling cross with the children now. They weren’t being nice to either Mr Green or Poppy. I saw that Viola and Emily weren’t happy as they both now stared at the ground and Jack looked close to tears. This wasn’t fun.

‘Well, it’s quite simple. Beneath the house that isn’t a house,’ Mr Green repeated. He sounded impatient.

‘I know, it’s under this caravan!’ Poppy exclaimed and she crawled on the floor, retrieving a bag of sweets.

‘Well done, Poppy.’ Mr Green smiled with relief.

As soon as he'd gone, Nathan and Stanley started laughing.

'That was such fun,' Nathan said.

'Why are you laughing?' Poppy asked.

'Well, you see before you arrived we decided to play a trick on Mr Green by not getting any of the clues right,' Stanley explained.

'You mean you did it on purpose?' Poppy said.

'Yes,' Viola said. 'It was Nathan's idea.' She looked embarrassed.

'I didn't want to do it – I like sweets,' Jack said. Emily patted his shoulder again.

'Well, I shan't be sharing with you, it wasn't nice,' Poppy said, clutching the sweets to her

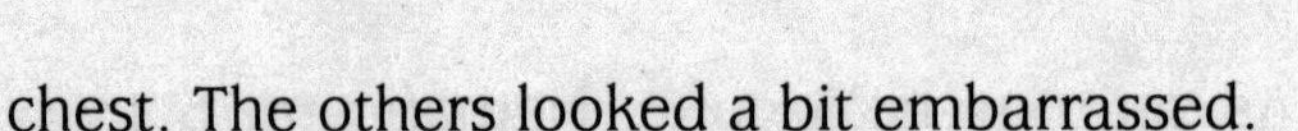

chest. The others looked a bit embarrassed.

'I'm sorry, we didn't mean to be mean,' Emily said.

'We really didn't,' Viola added. The two girls exchanged a shy smile.

'Don't worry, I'm sure we've got sweets in the van and I'll share them with all of you; even you, Poppy,' Stanley said. 'Come on.'

I started after them but a cat-shaped shadow loomed.

'Hello, Humphrey,' I said.

'What business did you have going on the treasure hunt?' he asked.

'I didn't know I wasn't allowed.'

'I am getting fed up with you being on my

territory.' He flicked his tail in anger. This was one mean cat.

'Look, one of my children, Viola, is unhappy, so I need to stay close to see if she's all right.'

'Um… Well I do like children, but I'd still prefer it if you could try to keep out of my way as much as possible.'

I bounded off. I didn't need asking twice.

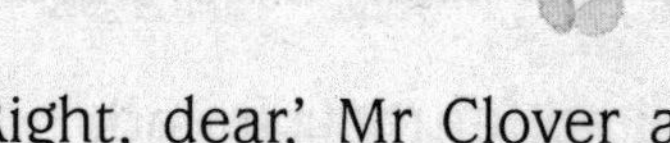

'Right, dear,' Mr Clover announced. He was wearing a rucksack, a big-brimmed hat and carrying a walking stick.

'What are you doing?' Mrs Clover asked. She was sitting in a chair with a big drawing pad on her lap.

'The children told me the treasure hunt was a bit of a disaster, so I am taking them on an adventure, to forage in the wood for fruit or whatever. We might even see a bear,' he laughed.

'Oh no!' Jack hid behind his sister.

'It'll be fine, young man, now go and tell your parents and meet me here as quick as you can.' Stanley and Viola were giggling excitedly as they waited for their friends.

'Viola,' Mrs Clover said. 'You need to do your piano now.'

'What?' Viola looked at her mother.

'Piano now. It's the only time the clubhouse is free.'

'But I was going with Dad and the others.' Her face fell.

'Nonsense, you can do that anytime – come along.'

I sat next to Viola on the piano stool. I had been desperate to go with the others but Viola needed me. Despite the fact that she was upset, she was playing beautifully.

'Oh, Alfie,' she said. She stopped playing and started stroking me. 'I do love the piano but I wish I could have gone with the others. If I can't make friends here, how will I ever manage at school?' She paused.

'Purr,' I said in understanding.

'I wish I was like Stanley – he makes friends so easily – but I really struggle and now I am in here on my own and they're off having fun. I'll never have any friends and I'll probably be on my own for ever!' She bashed the piano in frustration. I curled on to her lap to comfort her. She sighed and started playing again but I could see she was playing through tears.

That night, the children all sat round a table in the clubroom. I had snuck in again, getting better at this every day. They were still talking about foraging and what they had managed to collect, so Viola felt more left out than ever. No one noticed, but Emily kept shooting her worried glances. I nudged Viola but she didn't even look at Emily. She was intently staring at the table. I jumped on to her lap and she petted me. I also had a good view of the stage as a spotlight – which was actually Mrs Green holding a torch – shone on it and the curtains were pulled back to reveal Mr Green in a massive top hat and cloak, waving a magic wand. Everyone clapped, although Viola's was half-hearted.

'Welcome to my Magnificent Magic Show,' Mr Green said in a funny voice. 'I am Magician Green.' He took his hat off and put it on the table. Nathan rolled his eyes at Stanley.

'What?' Stanley whispered.

'This is going to be awful,' Nathan replied.

'Shush,' Poppy hissed.

'For my first trick, I shall join these silk scarves,' he announced with a flourish as he pulled a number of brightly coloured scarves out of his hat. He showed the audience how they were separate. Then he held them in one hand and waved his wand over them.

'Abracadabra,' he said, grabbing the end of one scarf; the rest fluttered to the floor.

'Oh dear,' he said, hurriedly picking them up. He tried again but the same thing happened. I saw Mrs Clover cover her mouth with her hand and Mr Clover's mouth twitched. The children all looked confused as Mr Green turned his back and hastily tied a few of them together. Despite the fact that we'd all seen him doing this, everyone clapped.

'Thank you, and now for the classic trick of pulling a rabbit out of a hat.'

My goodness, I thought, a rabbit? I wasn't sure I was keen on rabbits.

'But as we don't have a rabbit I am going to produce a cat from my hat.' Mr Green laughed as did everyone else. Viola looked at me. Mr Green showed the audience that the hat was empty, waved his wand over it and said his magic words. I heard a light laughter start from the adults and then Stanley and Nathan shouted.

'He's there!'

As Mr Green was looking in his empty hat, Humphrey had come round to the front of the stage and sat cleaning his paws. He yawned and then lay down.

‘What?’ Mr Green asked.

‘Humphrey – he’s on the stage!’ Nathan shouted and Mr Green looked over and, dithering for a moment, picked him up and shoved him into the hat.

‘MIAOW!’ Humphrey didn’t sound happy as he jumped straight out. The adults were all beside themselves with laughter now and I wasn’t sure whether to feel sorry for Mr Green or not.

‘For my final trick, I have a length of rope.’ He held it up. ‘I am going to cut it into three.’ He took some scissors and cut it. ‘Well, now, if we all say the magic words together it will rejoin.’ He looked hopefully at the audience.

'Right, one, two, three...'

'Abracadabra,' everyone shouted.

Mr Green closed his eyes and held up the end of the rope. He opened them to see the other two pieces flutter to the floor.

'That wasn't supposed to happen,' he said, looking crestfallen. Although Viola was still looking miserable, I put my paw on her arm, and she looked at me, then at poor Mr Green, and she started clapping loudly. Emily's eyes widened and she joined in. Then the rest of our table, except for Nathan, started cheering and the adults followed suit and Mr Green began to smile. Poor Mrs Green looked confused, though, as she kept the torch shining on her husband.

When it was quiet again, Emily turned to Viola.

'Well done – it was good you clapped, especially after the whole treasure hunt thing.'

Viola looked at me and smiled.

'Thanks, Emily, I felt we owed it to him,' Viola replied.

At least I knew what I needed to do. I needed to get Emily and Viola to become friends and then Viola would realise that she could easily make friends at her new school too. It sounded simple but I still had to figure out just how...

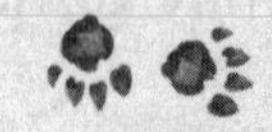

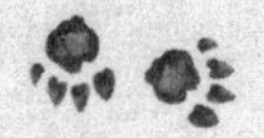
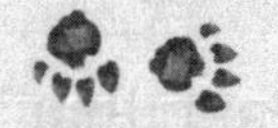

Chapter Four

I decided to take one of my nine lives in my paws and seek out Humphrey. I needed a friend and wanted to try to win grumpy Humphrey round. I found him cleaning his fur by the Greens' caravan.

'Good morning,' I said cheerfully.

'What do you want?' he asked.

'Viola is unhappy. She doesn't find it easy to make new friends. But, I have a plan to cheer her up.'

'A plan?'

'Yes, it's what I do and I need your help. Anyway, Emily, one of the other girls, she's a bit shy too and I think they would make lovely friends but I need to get them together.'

'How?'

'That's the thing – I'm not sure yet but I thought you might have some ideas.'

'Me?' Humphrey looked uncertain.

'I wouldn't ask if it wasn't important and it's not for me but for Viola.'

'Humph.' Humphrey didn't look happy. 'I will help with the girl…' He sounded reluctant.

That was as good as I could expect, and it had to be better than nothing, surely?

Help also came in the guise of Poppy. She was bossy and didn't like sharing but when it came to adults, she was always very nice. She even told Mr Green it was the best magic show she'd ever seen and I couldn't believe that was true.

I heard a knock on the van door; Mrs Clover opened it.

'Hello, Mrs Clover, it's a nice day, isn't it? I

like your hair, have you had it styled?' Poppy asked.

'Oh well, not really, dear; do come in.' Mrs Clover stood aside and patted her hair, which was a terrible mess as usual.

'Hi, Poppy,' Stanley said.

'I've organised a *Swingball* tournament,' Poppy told him.

'Is that an invitation or an order?' Stanley asked. I wasn't sure he liked Poppy.

'We'll just put our shoes on and come,' Viola said. She swatted Stanley on the arm.

I followed them over to Poppy's caravan; it was one of the best ones on the site, according to her, anyway. I had never seen a *Swingball* before – it was a pole with a string and a tennis ball attached. Poppy was brandishing two bats. Nathan, Jack and Emily were crowded round.

'Right, as I was explaining, the winner of each game will go on to play each other until we have a final winner. I'll play Jack, then the winner plays Stanley, then Emily, Nathan and Viola.'

'Does that make sense?' Stanley asked.

'No idea, but let's get on with it – we'll be here all vacation otherwise,' Nathan mumbled.

'Wow, you're good,' Jack said as, after failing to hit the ball more than once, Poppy was declared the winner of the first game.

Feeling like having a bit of fun, I jumped for the ball, missed it and slipped. Luckily, I managed to land on my feet.

'Yowl!' I cried. The children laughed.

'Alfie, we need to take this seriously,' Poppy said. So I leapt again. This time I managed to swipe the ball with my paw and everyone clapped.

'Right, Alfie, enough messing around, we really DO have to take this seriously,' Poppy said. She was SO bossy.

'Miaow!' I was having fun.

'Oh, let Alfie play. He's funny,' Stanley said.

'No, Stanley Clover, this is a serious game for people only.'

As I raised my tail in anger, I wondered if perhaps Poppy and Mr Green were related after all.

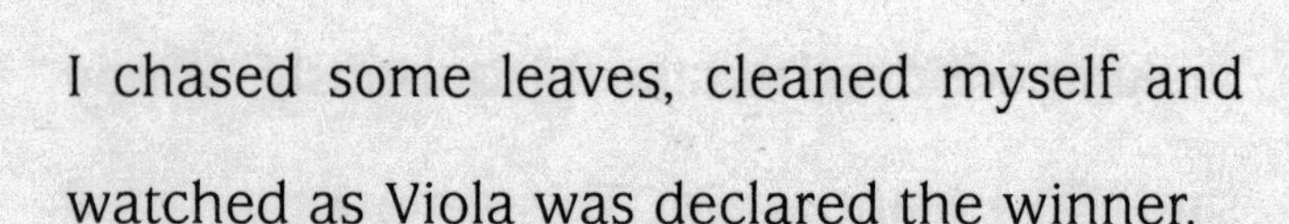

I chased some leaves, cleaned myself and watched as Viola was declared the winner.

'Wow, Vi, you were awesome,' Stanley said. I pricked my ears up. This should help her confidence.

'Yeah, I have to hand it to you – you beat me fair and square,' Nathan said good-naturedly.

'You were brilliant, Viola,' Emily stammered.

Viola beamed.

'The prize is that the winner gets to choose what we do next,' Poppy declared. 'So, Viola, it's up to you.'

'But that's no good – she'll only have to go and practise,' Stanley said. I wanted to cover my ears with my paws; that was the last thing Viola needed to hear. Viola looked upset and ran off.

'Stanley,' Emily said, voice barely above a whisper.

'What? What did I do?' Stanley asked, looking confused.

'OK, so Stanley, as her brother, then you get to choose,' Poppy decided.

'But shouldn't someone go after Viola?' Emily asked, but no one seemed to hear.

'It's called *Spyhunter*,' Stanley said as they all stood on the roundabout in the playground. Stanley was wearing a hat with flappy ears – one I often wore when Stanley dressed me up as his Adventurer's cat – and holding a magnifying glass. 'I'll be the hunter and you guys are all spies so you have to hide and I'll catch you.'

‘So, basically we are playing hide-and -seek,’ Poppy said.

‘No, we’re playing *Spyhunter*, it’s totally different. It’s an adventurer’s game,’ Stanley argued. He stood facing a tree trunk as Stanley counted to one hundred. Then he ran off; I struggled to keep up.

‘Ha, spy, got you,’ he said as he found Jack hiding under a bush, his bottom sticking out. I think it was the worst hiding I’d ever seen.

He managed to round up Poppy and Emily fairly quickly, so that just left Nathan. We all searched for him, looking everywhere we could think of, until the only place that remained was the clubhouse.

‘I’m going in,’ Stanley announced.

‘But we’re not allowed. Remember, Mr Green said we could only go in there with adult supervision.’ Emily looked worried. The other children agreed.

‘OK, you guys stay here and I’ll go.’ Stanley tried to look brave as he pushed open the door. I followed him inside. We looked under all the tables, by the small bar and even behind the piano but there was no sign of Nathan. Suddenly, we spotted a moving curtain, which hung behind the stage.

‘Ah ha, there he is,’ Stanley whispered and gesturing for me to be quiet, we made our way over. ‘Got you, spy,’ Stanley shouted triumphantly.

'You sure have.' Nathan smiled. He was sitting by a big box which seemed to have wooden people in it, attached to strings. I poked my nose into the box. I had never seen such things before. Just as I was about to take a closer look, 'PEEP!' I jumped and landed on my tail. Ouch.

'What are you two doing here?' Mr Green's voice boomed.

'Sorry, Uncle, we were playing hide—'

'I don't care – you shouldn't be here. Nathan, all you do is get into trouble, and as for you.' He pointed at Stanley. 'I just don't know. I shall be speaking to your parents. Now scram – I have my important puppet show tonight, so I need to concentrate on that. I'll work out what to do with you later.'

'Is everything all right?' Mrs Green appeared. She was holding a hammer. 'I've just come from fixing a shelf in the shop,' she explained.

'No, it is not.' Mr Green pointed at Nathan and Stanley.

'Oh, don't worry about that now. You need to be calm for your big show tonight. Come with me and I'll make you a nice cup of tea.' Mrs Green winked at the boys before leading him away.

'Now we've had it,' Stanley said.

'He might have to send me back to the States now,' Nathan said happily.

'So is that what this is all about?' said Stanley. 'It's all right for you, but I don't actually want to get thrown off the campsite – my parents will go mad.'

'Hey, calm down, I'll take the blame. Although you might change your mind when you have to sit through the worst puppet show in the world ever.'

'Is it that bad?'

'You thought his magic show was pretty crummy?' Nathan asked.

Stanley nodded.

'Well, this is a thousand times worse. Tonight is going to be the opposite of fun.' Nathan patted Stanley on the shoulder.

* * *

I could feel my fur tingle. I was thinking of a plan, and it was almost there. It was so brilliant. The puppets, Viola and the piano. In order to build Viola's confidence, what would be better than for her to play the piano in the clubhouse? But Mr Green had a monopoly on the entertainment – although I wasn't quite sure how entertaining he actually was – so how could it be achieved? I rushed off to find Humphrey.

He was outside one of the tents, eating as usual.

'Hello,' I said, trying to sound charming.

'What now?' Humphrey asked. He finished

eating and cleaned his whiskers.

'I really need your help. You see I have a plan to help Viola but I'm not sure how to go about it.' I outlined my idea.

'OK, so in order for your plan to work, we need to sabotage Mr Green's puppet show?'

Humphrey tilted his head, as if he was weighing it up. 'If it's for the girl, then I'll help. I've got a bit of a soft spot for her. Look, why don't we sneak into the clubhouse and hide the puppets.' As he explained the way my plan could work, I was overjoyed. It turned out Humphrey was quite a clever cat after all.

I lay on one of the benches in the van. It had been exhausting hiding the puppets. We had to get them in our mouths and drag them unseen to the place Humphrey chose – under the caravan. And now all I had to do was to get Viola to play the piano. I wasn't going to fail. Even Humphrey thought it could work.

I followed my family to the clubhouse that evening. I was trembling with nerves and excitement. This was it, my big moment to help Viola.

It was chaos. As everyone sat waiting for the entertainment, Mr Green was hysterical. His wife was trying to calm him down.

'Nathan, are you sure you didn't take my puppets?' Mr Green asked.

'No, Uncle. As soon as we left the clubhouse I went with Stanley to help his dad get food for supper.'

The Clovers approached.

'What seems to be the matter?' Mr Clover asked.

‘I was supposed to perform my puppet show this evening, but somehow my puppets have disappeared. These boys were the last to see them.’ Mr Green pointed at Nathan and Stanley. Oops, I hadn’t thought about the boys getting into trouble.

‘Stanley, do you know anything about this?’ Mr Clover asked.

‘No, I really absolutely don’t. Dad, we’ve been with you all afternoon.’ Stanley stated.

‘Yes, that’s true; Mr Green actually Nathan was most helpful.’

‘What are we going to do?’ Mr Green shrieked. ‘We have a clubhouse full of people who need entertaining.’

It was my big moment. Humphrey was sitting by the door. He raised his tail. I ran over to the piano, sat on the stool, raised my paw and bashed some keys.

'Look,' Jack said, pointing. 'Alfie the cat is playing the piano.' He laughed.

I jumped on to the keys and tried to play more. Now everyone was laughing. Then, as I planned, Viola came and joined me. She stroked me, sat down beside me and started to play. As the most beautiful music filled the clubhouse, everyone was silent. When she finished her song, she stood up.

'Oh no, please carry on,' Mrs Green said. 'I've never heard such wonderful playing.'

'Humph,' Mr Green said. 'And that cat is not supposed to be here.'

'Oh, one night won't hurt. Please, Viola?' Mrs Green said.

'But...' Viola stammered.

'Go on, Vi, you're the best piano prodigy ever,' Stanley shouted and then the audience started chanting.

'MORE, MORE, MORE.' Viola blushed and smiled shyly at me. I gave her my most reassuring look, and tickled her with my tail.

When Viola finished, everyone was standing up, clapping and cheering. Her cheeks were flushed pink and she was beaming. My plan had worked. As the evening drew to a close and everyone started to leave, she was congratulated over and over.

Emily hovered. 'Wow, you are so good,' she muttered.

'Thank you,' Viola blushed.

'Maybe tomorrow, I mean, if it's OK, can I come and watch you practise?' Emily asked.

'I'd love that.' Viola's smile stretched across her whole face and so did my grin.

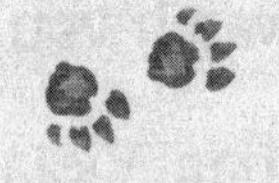

Chapter Five

I heard soft footsteps. Luckily my hearing is amazing, being a cat. I got up from where I'd been sleeping and spotted a shadowy figure: Stanley. He was quietly gathering food, putting it in a bag. What was he up to? No one else woke. Mr Clover was snoring –

he sounded like a very noisy train, and if Mrs Clover and Viola could sleep through that, nothing would wake them. I crept out of the van after Stanley; I had a bad feeling.

He made his way through the dark, using his torch, to the edge of the woods. I was surprised to see the rest of the children already there. They were wearing jumpers over their pyjamas as they laid out a rug and piled up snacks.

'Our midnight feast,' Nathan announced.

'With ghost stories,' Stanley added.

'It's going to be sooo cool!' Jack said excitedly.

'I know a really good story,' Poppy said in

her bossy voice.

'Where's Viola?' Emily asked.

'Oh. Oh dear, I forgot to tell her, what with so much going on,' Stanley said. He hung his head.

'Can't you go and get her?' Poppy suggested.

'No way – if I go back, I might wake everyone up and then we'll be in trouble. I'm really sorry, I didn't mean to forget her.'

'Right, I'm going to tell the first story,' Nathan said, as he shone a torch at his face.

'You look spooky,' Jack said, snuggling closer to his sister.

'Once there was this old house in the middle of a forest—' Nathan started.

'What was that?' Jack almost jumped on to Emily's lap.

'I think it came from the wood; what is it?' Poppy asked.

'You don't think it's a bear?' Jack asked.

'Can I get on with my story?' Nathan said, but a bright torch shone in the distance.

'It's Mr Green!' Stanley exclaimed.

'RUN!' Nathan shouted.

I wasn't sure who to follow as they all ran off in different directions. I went after

Stanley, who had followed Poppy. Mr Green was getting nearer, and I heard an almighty scream. Poppy was lying on the ground on top of a tent which she had managed to pull down. The people staying in the tent were trying to crawl out.

'What on earth is going on?' they screeched. Poppy burst into tears. Stanley went to help her and Mr Green appeared in his stripy pyjamas. Mrs Green ran up behind him.

'What is happening?' he bellowed. The commotion from the tent had woken the whole campsite and when I saw everyone coming out of their caravans, tents and vans, I knew we were in big trouble.

'What on earth is going on, Stanley?' Mrs Clover shouted as she, Mr Clover and Viola approached.

'We thought we'd have a midnight feast,' Stanley started.

'It was my idea,' Nathan admitted.

'I got scared,' Jack piped up. Emily was holding his hand. 'I think there's a grizzly bear in the wood.'

'Midnight feasts are against the rules. Rule 378 to be precise,' Mr Green stated.

The adults looked sleepy and cross.

'Stanley, I despair of you. At least Viola was sensible and didn't go,' Mrs Clover said.

'I wasn't invited,' Viola shouted. She turned

and ran back to the van.

'Right, well, I have to help these poor people put their tent back up,' Mrs Green said, holding a mallet.

'Nathan, you go straight to bed, and as for the rest of you, I've a good mind to throw you out,' Mr Green shouted.

'Mr Green,' Mrs Clover said. 'I really am sorry and I promise that I'll punish Stanley, and I'm sure the other parents will tell their children off too, but please let us stay – we are having such a wonderful holiday.'

'Yes, it's the nicest campsite we've ever been to,' Poppy's dad added. Soon all the adults were begging Mr Green for another chance.

‘I shall sleep on it tonight and we’ll see,’ Mr Green huffed.

As the children were taken off to bed and the adults returned to where they were sleeping, I was wondering how a holiday could be so exhausting…

My triumph with Viola and the piano-playing was short-lived. The following morning, everyone was tired and grumpy with each other.

‘Vi, I’m really sorry, I didn’t mean to leave you out but I just forgot.’

‘Great, so you can forget I exist. What am I, the invisible sister? I know why I’ll never make any friends in my new school – no one ever even remembers me.' She had tears in her eyes.

'That's not—'

'Stop talking to me, Stan.' I had never heard Viola so cross.

I went to see the rest of the children, but they were all miserable and being kept a close eye on so I sought out Humphrey who was lying beside the clubhouse, in a sunny spot.

'Hello,' I said.

'What's wrong with you?' he asked.

'The kids are in trouble again. Everyone's miserable and I'm back to square one.'

'Yes, I heard. Mr Green was raging about it this morning. Mrs Green had to give him four sausages to calm him down!'

'He threatened to throw us out.'

'He won't, though, Mrs Green will see to that.'

'I just don't know what to do. I thought I'd helped Viola but now, with her being left out, she's upset again!'

'Humans aren't as clever as us cats, which is the problem. Look, why don't I give you a tour of my favourite spots? Maybe it'll help you come up with ideas.' I was startled. Was Humphrey actually being nice to me?

'But don't get any ideas. I'm only doing what any decent cat would do,' he added.

We sat under one of the fattest bushes I'd ever seen. As I swiped at a fly and pulled on some leaves, I did start to feel better. We'd been almost round the whole campsite, and very pleasant it had been too.

'The thing is, Alfie, that Viola is worried about her new school and making friends, and this holiday is making it worse because she hasn't been able to join in,' said Humphrey.

'Yeah, the piano practice. Her parents make her do it when the others are having fun. If she practised early in the morning then she's free all day, but no one seems to have thought of that.'

'It's a bit late now. You've only got a couple of days left. But if she could be more involved with the other children, even at this late stage, she might feel better about starting school.'

'Exactly. Which is why I thought last night was such a good idea. Emily reached out to her but the midnight feast ruined everything.'

'Hmmm, it's not an easy one. Let's go to the playground, I'll show you my favourite tree. It's not too high, before you start getting funny.'

I sat on a low branch; Humphrey was above me. It was such a lovely day and we could see much of the campsite. The Clovers were sitting outside the van; they didn't look happy, even from here.

'Look,' Humphrey said. 'I think you're right – we need to get Viola and Emily to be friends.'

'But how?' I asked.

'We've got the rest of today to come up with something. Let's meet in the morning. Right now I need something to eat.' He ran down the tree with ease and I followed him, a little more slowly.

'It's been a great tour; thanks for agreeing to help.'

'I told you, it's for the girl, not you.'

I went back to the van to be met by an angry Mrs Clover.

'Where have you been? Don't you think I've got enough to worry about without losing you? Goodness, Alfie, you're almost as bad as Stanley.'

As I slunk inside in disgrace, I joined Stanley and Viola, who were sulking, and I sulked right along with them.

That evening, Mr and Mrs Clover took the children to the clubhouse as usual.

'I thought we had to stay in,' Stanley said.

'Mr Green wants everyone there to watch his puppet show,' Mr Clover explained. 'And after what happened, it's the very least we can do.' Ah, Humphrey said he'd found the puppets. 'Now come along.'

It seemed that the puppet show was going to be our punishment, as Stanley plonked me on his lap to watch.

The stage was set up with what Stanley

explained was a puppet theatre. Mr Green was behind it and we could see two puppets covered by a curtain. I wasn't sure if this was how it was supposed to be but I could see the strings and Mr Green's sleeves flapping away.

'Hello,' a high-pitched voice which seemed to belong to a girl puppet said. Ah, I got it, Mr Green was doing the voices. The girl puppet moved across the stage. 'I'm Little Red Riding Hood and I'm visiting my grandma with a basket of fruit.'

THUD. A basket appeared through the curtain and fell on the floor.

'Oops,' Mr Green's voice said before he

remembered himself. 'Oops,' he said again in the girl's voice. Mrs Green rushed on to the stage and handed the basket back through to her husband. The girl disappeared and in her place came something that looked like an ugly dog.

'Hello, children.' The voice wasn't that dissimilar to the little girl, although a bit meaner. 'I am the Big Bad Wolf, I am going to Grandma's house and I'm going to eat her up.'

I snuggled into Stanley's lap. I was a bit scared.

'Oh boy,' Nathan said as the wolf then got tangled in the curtain and clattered to the

floor. Mrs Green ran on to the stage again, picked him up and quickly gave him to Mr Green.

Things went properly wrong when the wolf met Grandma, an old lady puppet.

'Hello, I am here to eat you up,' the wolf said as the wolf puppet collided with Grandma.

CRASH. BANG.

'Ouch,' Mr Green's voice said as the puppets disappeared. We all watched in horror as the wooden puppet theatre slowly tipped backwards and fell.

'Ahhhhh, help,' Mr Green cried.

Mrs Green rushed forward, as did Mr and Mrs Clover. As they lifted the puppet theatre, we saw Mr Green tangled up in the puppets' string. Mrs Green pulled off her tool belt and set to work, finally freeing Mr Green.

The room was silent. No one knew whether to laugh or cry; even the children looked shocked. Mr Green shook his head and walked off and Mrs Green was left standing there.

'Sorry, folks, things do go wrong sometimes, but I hope you all had a good evening, and goodnight.'

It was a glum end to a glum day and the children weren't allowed to play together as they were all marched off to bed.

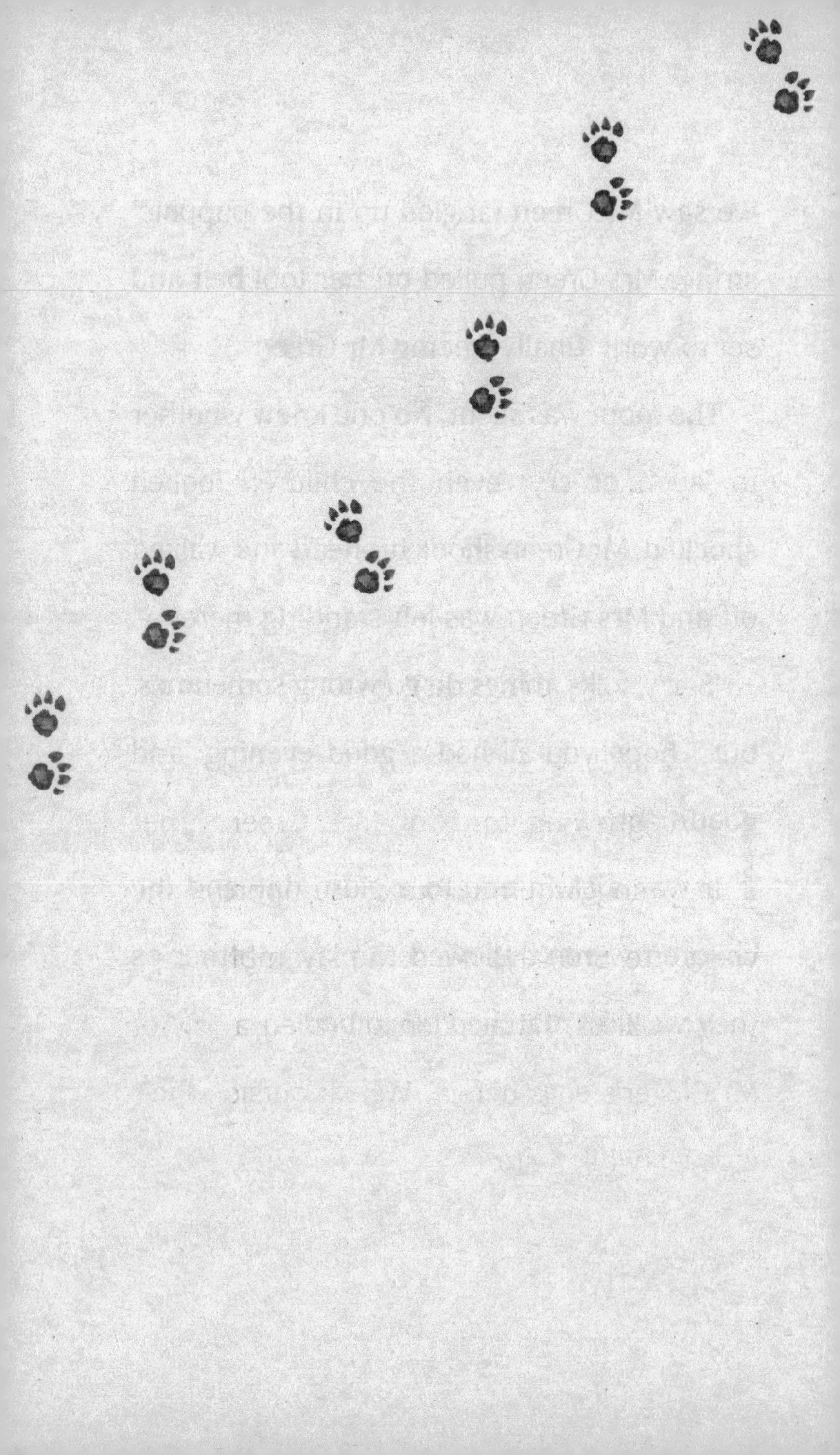

Chapter Six

I was growing fond of Mrs Green. That morning when I found Humphrey, she was there. She gave me some scrambled egg, which I liked; I'd accidentally tried a few of Mr Clover's eggs before. We sat outside their caravan while I ate.

'How are things today?' he asked.

'Better. But not great. Viola's still sad.'

'That's bad.'

'I know, she was so upset at being left out of the midnight feast.'

'Oh, by the way.' Humphrey scratched behind his ears. 'I heard Mrs Green telling Mr Green that instead of throwing all the children out, they should give them a project to do. My suggestion is you keep an eye on them, and look for opportunities.'

'I like your thinking. What about you?'

'I need to do my campsite rounds and then take a nap. Alfie, remember Mr Green doesn't like you being here, so try to keep a low profile.'

'Thanks, Humphrey, you are being great about all this.'

'Yes, but don't forget—'

'I know – it's not for me, it's for Viola.'

'Exactly.' But as he grinned, I knew I was cracking this cat.

Mr Green rounded everyone up. 'We're having a big picnic on your last day.'

The children cheered. 'Yes, well, no need for that. Rule 244 states no unwarranted overexcitement.'

'What does that mean?' Jack asked; Emily gave him a gentle kick.

'As I was saying, we have a picnic for the whole campsite which we hold over there at the edge of the woods.' He pointed to the clearing that Humphrey and I explored yesterday.

'So what can we do?' Mrs Clover asked.

'Well, my wife suggested that the children could make some decorations for the picnic. In the clubhouse we have materials to make bunting for the trees, and we have lots of baskets to decorate. What do you think?'

'I think it's an excellent idea, Mr Green, and will definitely keep them out of trouble,' Mr Clover laughed.

'Right, well, good. I'll leave you all to go

directly to the clubhouse and get creative.' Mr Green blew his whistle.

I felt pleased by the turn of events as I followed the children to the clubhouse. Stanley and Nathan ran in and straight up to the table where Mr Green had put the craft supplies; Jack tried to keep up with them. Poppy, Emily and Viola followed.

'I know all about bunting so I should be in charge of that,' Poppy said.

'What's bunting?' Nathan asked.

'Sort of like flags, tied together, that you hang up,' Poppy explained. 'Anyway, I'll make it.'

‘I can help you,’ Jack said eagerly. Poppy nodded.

‘What shall we do?’ Stanley said. Nathan shrugged.

‘I know, why don’t you paint a sign saying *Curly Wood’s Picnic 2016*,’ Viola suggested quietly.

‘Hey, not a bad idea,’Nathan said. I felt a tingling in my fur again.

This was what I needed. Viola was really creative, so I just needed

to nudge her forward a bit. I jumped on her lap to give her confidence.

'Miaow,' I said loudly. Viola giggled.

'Viola is so good at stuff like this,' Stanley said; she blushed.

It worked, Viola was gaining confidence as she directed the children, quietly and kindly, ideas flowing. She helped Poppy and Jack make different-coloured bunting and even suggested painting the American flag on some of them

in honour of Nathan. Then she and Emily started decorating baskets with flowers and ribbons. They started talking more; I was beside myself with happiness as they giggled and chatted happily.

'We live in Bristol. It's nice there but I have been to London once,' Emily said.

'We've just moved there – I have to go to music school,' Viola explained.

'Well, you are brilliant.'

'Thanks, but it's scary starting a new school and I was sad to leave my friends. I miss them.' Viola smiled sadly.

'You can always make new friends, though,' Emily said.

Just then there was a commotion; we all looked over to where Nathan and Stanley were flicking paint at each other.

'Yelp!' I went over to them crossly; this was not a time for getting into trouble. Emily and Viola exchanged a look.

'YOWL.' I felt my legs slip beneath me as I skidded on some paint. BUMP! I landed on my bottom and flew head-first into a table. Then I could only watch in horror as a pot of paint jumped from the table. SPLAT! The sticky green paint slowly rolled down my fur.

'Whoops, sorry, I didn't mean to make Alfie slip over,' Nathan looked upset.

'Oh, Alfie!' Viola shouted, rushing over, although she didn't touch me.

'What have you done?' Poppy shouted. 'Now we'll be in trouble again.'

'It was an accident,' Stanley said.

'Alfie's green!' Jack exclaimed.

I ran round in circles. It seemed I was in for a bath and I really hated baths.

'I know – there's a sink in the back room,' Nathan suggested. 'If we clean him in there, maybe no one will know?'

'But it's paint. It doesn't just come off easily and it's all in his fur!' Poppy sounded more distressed than I was.

‘Dad has that stuff that cleans paint off his hands. It must be safe to use on fur if you can use it on skin,’ Viola said.

‘But is it safe for cats?’ Emily asked.

‘It doesn’t say so on the bottle, but then they probably don’t have to get paint off many cats,’ Stanley pointed out.

‘It’ll be fine, said Viola. Look, Stanley, take Alfie into the sink. Nathan, you go with him. Poppy and Jack, keep watch for Mr Green and if he appears, distract him, and Emily, we can go to the van and get the cleaner.’

I was impressed, if not still annoyed, as Viola mobilised the troops. I realised that this girl had so much going for her – she was talented, creative and clever so why didn't she see what I saw?

I went to find Humphrey. Yet again, I needed help. It was as if we took a paw forward and then a paw backwards when it came to solving problems. At least I was no longer green, although the scrubbing took a bit more effort than I would have liked and I smelt funny. Humphrey was eating some fine-looking sardines outside a holidaymaker's tent. No wonder he didn't want me around.

'Hi,' I said sadly.

'Oh boy, what now?'

'It was all going so well, Viola was brilliant at making the decorations for the picnic, but then...' I told him about the paint incident.

'I wish I'd seen that,' he chortled.

'Well, anyway, back to the problem.' I gave him a look. 'The thing is that they cleaned me up, and they were laughing and all getting along but then Mrs Clover arrived and said she was organising the children to decorate the picnic baskets to keep them out of trouble.'

'Get to the point, Alfie, I've got fish to finish.'

'They were all excited, but then Mrs Clover

told Viola that she had to practise her piano.'

'Oh.'

'And Viola begged her to let her do it later, but Mrs Clover said it was impossible because Mr Green had to set up for Bingo, and that she could do picnic baskets later.'

'Viola's feeling left out again?'

'Yes, just as she and Emily were getting close.'

'Poor kid.'

'So what am I going to do?'

'I'm not sure Alfie, but hey, look, we will come up with something, and in the meantime why don't you share some of my sardines. You look like you need cheering up.'

Maybe Humphrey was my friend after all.

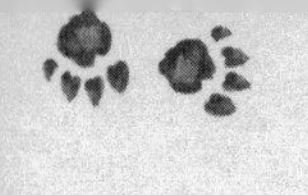

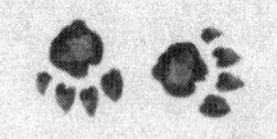

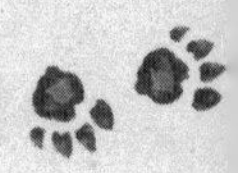

Chapter Seven

'No, we can't do that,' Emily was saying. What?

I was trying to listen in to the children in the playground.

'Come on, it'll be so cool,' Nathan said. 'It's boring here. We'll go to the woods, find the place where Stanley's dad took us and see if we can spot any bears.'

'There are no bears,' Poppy said.

'Well, come with us to find out for sure,' Nathan challenged.

'But we'll get in so much trouble,' Emily complained.

'No one will know we've even gone, they're so busy getting ready for the picnic,' Nathan argued.

'I know; as an adventurer I've got a very good idea. I'll go and get some peanuts and we can leave a trail so we definitely absolutely won't get lost,' Stanley suggested.

'Well, I'm not going and, Jack, you shouldn't

either,' Emily said.

'But, but…' Jack looked at the older boys.

'YOWL,' I shouted. I was with Emily.

'Oh, Alfie, it'll be fine.' Stanley patted my head and ran off.

After they left, Emily was alone. She was upset and so was I. Those children really shouldn't have gone into the woods, and goodness knows what Mr Green would do when he found out. I had to act fast, so I went to find Viola.

As soon as I spotted her I yowled, and howled and yelped with all my might.

'Goodness, Alfie, whatever is wrong?'

I headed for the playground; she followed

me and found Emily crying.

'What's wrong, Em?' she asked, putting her arm round her friend.

'They've all gone to the woods – to the place where your dad took us the other day.'

'What?' Viola was concerned.

'What are we going to do?' Emily asked.

'Hope they come back before anyone notices?' Viola suggested.

Not really what I was thinking but, hey, I could go with that.

Emily and Viola looked worried as they wandered about the campsite. Every time they saw one of the adults they had to keep dodging questions about where the others were.

'Lunchtime,' Mrs Clover shouted finally. 'Where's Stanley?'

'I think he's having lunch with Nathan,' Viola said quickly.

After lunch they still weren't back. Viola and Emily were worried.

'What do you think can have happened to them?' said Emily.

'I hope they haven't got lost,' said Viola.

I went to find Humphrey. He was sunbathing. 'We have to go to the wood,' I said.

'What? Why?' Humphrey listened as I explained. 'But how will we know where to find them? The wood's massive.'

Ah, I hadn't thought of that. But then I had a brainwave. 'Emily – she went with Mr Clover, she might know.'

We ran off to find the girls, who were back in the playground. 'Hurry up, we have to get going.'

'We need to tell our parents,' Viola was saying, as they stood by the swings.

'They'll be in so much trouble,' Emily said.

'But I don't know what else to do.'

I made as much noise as I could, even making Humphrey jump, and as the girls looked at me I ran off in the direction of the wood.

'No, Alfie,' Viola shouted, but I ran as fast as I could, Humphrey beside me, and the girls had no choice but to follow.

Sometimes, I need to think out my plans more clearly. I was in the wood but had no idea which direction to go in. I then stopped and looked around; Humphrey was calmly sitting next to me. I ran round in circles, unable to get my bearings, before I tripped on a stick.

'Yelp.'

'Oh, Alfie.' Viola scooped me up. Humphrey made a face and Emily looked worried. 'What are we going to do?'

'I guess, now we're in the wood, we could find them,' Emily said tentatively. 'I remember the way we went. It's not far.'

'OK, we don't really have a choice,' Viola said, setting me down on the ground. We all set off.

'I'm not sure this was your best idea,' Humphrey said grumpily; the ground was very uncomfortable.

'You didn't have to come,' I pointed out.

'Who else will save you from trouble?'

I muttered under my breath, 'What trouble?'

The uneven ground crackled underneath my paws, which made me uneasy. From up above came rustling sounds and strange-sounding bird noises. It was a little scary. I soon decided the woods weren't my favourite ever place, as shadows loomed; it went from dark to light in an instant and I felt more and more nervous. I stumbled on yet another stone and tried to regain my balance.

'YELP!' I jumped as a furry thing with a bushy tail stood in front of me. I started trembling.

'It's just a squirrel, Alfie,' Humphrey laughed, as he walked past it.

Before long we spotted them; they were clinging to a tree.

'What are you doing?' Viola shouted breathlessly, as we reached them.

'Well, you see there was a bear,' Jack started.

'You saw a bear?' Emily asked. I had a quick glance around. I hoped it wasn't still here.

'Not exactly but we sure heard one,' Nathan said.

'You see, we left a trail of peanuts, so we'd be able to find our way back,' Stanley explained. 'And we got here and carved our names on the tree trunk, did some adventuring and started to go back but the peanuts had been eaten.

We heard a bear so we were all hugging this tree for safety.'

'I'm hungry,' Poppy cried.

'I don't think there's a bear,' Viola said sensibly. 'In fact, I am sure you can't get bears in these parts.'

'But a bear must have eaten the peanuts,' Jack said; he was trembling.

'You'll find that was the squirrels,' Viola said. 'There's loads of them.'

I could vouch for that.

'Come on, let's go – we'll get you home. Emily's so good at directions,' Viola said.

'Thanks.' Emily was pink. 'And hopefully no one will know you were missing.'

But as I looked at them, covered in dirt, I was pretty sure they would.

Sure enough, Mr and Mrs Green and all the adults were standing by the playground when we got back. I was tired; it had been a long walk. Humphrey went to stand behind Mrs Green.

'Where on earth have you been?' Mr Green shouted.

Nathan hung his head. 'We went to the woods.'

'Without an adult?'

Nathan nodded.

'You have broken rules 3, 7,10, 17, and, well, just about every rule in the book.' He looked very cross, as Mrs Green put her hand on her husband's arm; but even she looked angry.

'It was my idea,' Nathan admitted.

'Stanley, you should have known better,' Mrs Clover bellowed. 'We were worried, worried sick.'

'Sorry, Mum. We weren't going to be long but we kind of got lost. Viola and Emily rescued us,' Stanley said. Everyone looked at Viola and Emily.

'That's all well and good but you should have come to get us.' Mr Green blew his whistle.

'We were going to,' Viola said, her voice barely above a whisper. 'But then Alfie ran into the wood, so we had to go after him, then Emily remembered where they went with Dad.'

'Ah, I see,' Mrs Green said.

'And Em wouldn't come with us in the first place. She told us we shouldn't go,' Jack added.

'Good girl, Emily,' her father said.

'Right, well, girls, you deserve a reward. You can have pizza in the clubhouse tonight,' Mrs Green said.

'But the rest of you – you should really all

be thrown off the campsite, the amount of rules you've broken,' Mr Green added.

'But tomorrow is their last day,' Mrs Green pointed out. 'And we've got the picnic so they can't get into any more trouble. Nathan, go to the caravan and stay there.'

Mr Green looked as if he was going to argue but he didn't.

All the other children were grounded, so I went with Viola and Emily to the clubhouse that night. Outside, Humphrey was eating tuna; he gestured to a second bowl.

'That's for you. A reward for rescuing the kids,' he said, and we shared a pleasant dinner together.

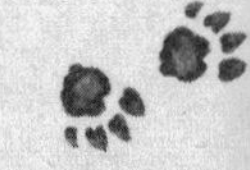

Chapter Eight

We woke to pouring rain and everyone worrying about the picnic.

Stanley was busy trying to be good; Viola was reading and Mr and Mrs Clover were chatting about what they were going to do when they got home, when there was a knock on the door. Mr Green, wearing an enormous coat and hat, stood outside. He looked cheerful. I wondered if it was because it was our last day.

'I won't come in, I'll drip all over your van, but Mrs Green and I had a chat and we thought that we'd move the picnic into the clubhouse. The children can go over and get decorating.'

Both Stanley and Viola perked up at that. As they put on raincoats and left the van, I braved the weather and went with them. I shook myself off as I went inside. The others were already there, but they didn't seem very happy.

'Hi,' Stanley said cheerfully. The others grumbled their response.

'Shall we start decorating now?' Viola suggested.

'Not with him,' Poppy said, pointing at Nathan.

'Why?' Viola asked.

'All week he's been trying to get us into trouble. My parents took away my pocket money,' Poppy explained.

'And mine were very cross,' Jack added.

'It's true you really have got us all in trouble,' Stanley pointed out. Nathan looked at everyone, then stomped off.

'Miaow.' I ran after him; he went to the backstage room, sat on one of the boxes and crossed his arms. I felt sorry for him, although he did keep getting them into trouble, but it was because he was unhappy. I jumped up on to a box next to him. He stroked me sadly.

'No one likes me any more,' he said to me. I purred and nestled into him.

After a while, Viola appeared.

'Nathan, are you all right?' Viola asked.

'Everyone hates me,' he said.

'No, they don't, they're just upset. You have to admit that saying it would be OK to go to the woods was a bit dumb.'

'Yeah, real dumb. The thing is, I've been

so homesick that I thought that if I caused a bit of trouble my uncle and aunt might send me back.'

I rubbed his arm.

'I didn't know... You are a long way from home.'

'Yeah, I've never been away from my parents for this long. I mean, it's nice of them to have me to stay and it was exciting going on a plane on my own and England is nice, but I miss my parents and my friends back home.'

'I understand. We moved house a little while before we came here, and I had to say goodbye to all my friends.'

I also understood. I was missing my home, Edgar Road, although I was so busy I didn't have much time to be homesick.

'So you know how it feels?'

'Yes and so would the others if you explained it to them.'

'I will; thanks, Viola. You know I've had a great time this week with you all. That's why I don't want them to be mad at me.'

'It's been nice to meet you,' Viola said, smiling.

'You too. You're cool for a girl, Viola. I mean you play the piano so well and you won *Swingball,* then how you made the decorations... You basically organised the whole thing, not to mention rescuing us.'

'I did?' Viola sounded surprised.

'Hey, maybe you don't realise how cool you are.' Nathan jumped down from the box and went to talk to the others.

Viola was smiling; how brilliant was it that Nathan had said exactly what I was thinking?

Viola was more confident as she helped everyone decorate the hall. Nathan had said sorry and everyone was friends again. I noticed that Emily and Viola seemed to be really close. My heart swelled with joy. And when we left the clubhouse to go back to the van, the rain had almost stopped.

I saw Humphrey.

'Hello,' I said.

'So, you're leaving tomorrow?'

'Yes. I've had a nice time but I'm looking forward to going back.'

'Everything OK with the girl?'

'Yes, that's the best bit. She seems so much happier now. The rescue pushed her and Emily together, so thanks for your help.'

'I would say it was a pleasure but having to go into the woods, hide the puppets and everything else, was a lot of work. I won't be sorry to see you go.'

Did he really say that? I saw Viola approach out of the corner of my eye and

I turned to Humphrey.

'Do you have to be so mean?' I asked. I then hissed at him to show how angry I was.

'Whoa, calm down,' he replied.

'No, Humphrey, I've been nothing but nice to you. I didn't try to take the attention off you with the humans; I didn't steal your food; I was respectful of the fact that I was on your territory and yet still you can say mean things?' I hissed again.

'Alfie, are you fighting?' Viola asked, looking worried. I turned to her, then scowled at Humphrey. Humphrey stared at me; I held his gaze. I wasn't a pushover after all. As we stared at each other for what seemed like ages, I wondered if he would in fact pounce on me. I felt my fur trembling as I tried to hold my nerve but then, Humphrey stretched his tail in a friendly gesture.

'Meow,' he said. He was calling a truce. I blinked slowly at him as he whispered an apology, which I accepted. I wasn't a cat to hold grudges. And I also felt relieved – he was bigger than me after all.

'Viola,' Mrs Clover said.

'Yes, Mum?'

'It's time for your piano practice.'

Mr Clover and Stanley stood beside her.

'But we're getting ready for the picnic; I'm meeting Emily.'

'Well, you can do that later. Piano first.' Viola was about to go but then she looked at me.

I rubbed her legs.

'No, Mum, no. I have missed playing with the others all week because of piano and I haven't complained but now I have one day left so the piano can wait.'

I purred with pride.

‘But Viola—’

‘You know how worried I’ve been about making friends at my new school.’ Viola was quietly spoken but very firm; we weren’t used to her sounding quite so assertive.

Mrs Clover looked at Mr Clover, who shrugged.

‘Miaow,’ I said in agreement.

‘I’m sorry, I got it wrong, Viola, but I thought you loved the piano.’

‘I do, Mum, and I’m happy to practise but I am old enough to decide *when* and you never let me.’

Mrs Clover grabbed Viola in a hug. ‘I’m sorry, it seems I have underestimated you;

you should be with your friends today.'

'Right, good, then I'm going to find Emily.'

Mr and Mrs Clover and Stanley all looked as Viola walked off and I am pretty sure they were impressed.

Everyone from the campsite sat on blankets in the clubhouse enjoying the picnic. The children were complimented on what a great job they'd done with the decorations and even Mr Green smiled. Humphrey and I were allowed into the clubhouse and given lots of treats.

'You are lucky being a campsite cat,' I said to him.

'Thanks, Alfie, and I'm sorry I haven't been as nice as I could be. I'll even miss you a bit when you go.'

We were friends, Viola had made friends and had found her confidence, so all in all it had been a very successful holiday.

* * *

As we set off the following day, everyone was sad to be leaving. Emily and Viola said they would keep in touch and Nathan even promised to write from America. Nathan had spoken to his parents the previous evening and he said it had made him feel much better, thanks to his new friends. Stanley even let Poppy almost hug him and Jack cried. Even Mr Green had tears in his eyes but they may have been tears of joy.

We all settled down in the van for the long drive home.

'Can we come back here next year?' Viola asked.

'I don't see why not,' Mrs Clover said.

'And Alfie too?' Stanley asked.

'If his family agree,' Mr Clover said.

Viola and Stanley cheered and I curled up to have a catnap; I was happy to come back but at the same time I was glad I had a year to recover from this holiday.

Have you read: